Dancing in My Bones

by Sylvia Andrews
pictures by Ellen Mueller

HarperFestival®
A Division of HarperCollinsPublishers

I've got dancing in my bones, in my bones.
I've got dancing in my bones, in my bones.
I've got hip-hopping, tip-topping,
be-bopping, no-stopping
dancing in my bones, in my bones.

I've got tapping in my feet, in my feet.
I've got tapping in my feet, in my feet.
I've got hip-hopping, tip-topping,
be-bopping, no-stopping
tapping in my feet, in my feet.

I've got bouncing in my knees, in my knees.
I've got bouncing in my knees, in my knees.
I've got hip-hopping, tip-topping,
be-bopping, no-stopping
bouncing in my knees, in my knees.

I've got swaying in my hips, in my hips.
I've got swaying in my hips, in my hips.
I've got hip-hopping, tip-topping,
be-bopping, no-stopping
swaying in my hips, in my hips.

I've got snapping in my fingers, in my fingers.
I've got snapping in my fingers, in my fingers.
I've got hip-hopping, tip-topping,
be-bopping, no-stopping
snapping in my fingers, in my fingers.

I've got clapping in my hands, in my hands.
I've got clapping in my hands, in my hands.
I've got hip-hopping, tip-topping,
be-bopping, no-stopping
clapping in my hands, in my hands.

I've got shaking in my shoulders, in my shoulders.
I've got shaking in my shoulders, in my shoulders.
I've got hip-hopping, tip-topping,
be-bopping, no-stopping
shaking in my shoulders, in my shoulders.

I've got music in my head, in my head.
I've got music in my head, in my head.
I've got hip-hopping, tip-topping,
be-bopping, no-stopping
music in my head, in my head.

I've got singing in my mouth, in my mouth.
I've got singing in my mouth, in my mouth.
I've got hip-hopping, tip-topping,
be-bopping, no-stopping
singing in my mouth, in my mouth.

I've got dancing in my heart, in my heart.
I've got dancing in my heart, in my heart.
I've got hip-hopping, tip-topping,
be-bopping, no-stopping
dancing in my heart, in my heart.
Yes...a WHOLE LOT of dancing in my heart.